JUMBO JILL AND SLIM JACK

A BBW (Big Beautiful Woman) High School Romance between Best Friends

Elizabeth Biggum

CONTENTS

JUMBO JILL AND SLIM JACK

CHAPTER 1

It was a cloudy afternoon when the moving truck stopped in front of 252 Sunny Lane. A car parked right behind it, and a woman got down from the passenger seat, opening the back door and fumbling around.

"Hurry, mummy, I need to wee!" a little voice said from inside.

"If you stay still, then I will be able to undo your seatbelt!" the woman yelled, a little annoyed after the long drive.

As soon as the seat belt was off, the little boy ran out of the car and straight into the tree in the front yard. He sighed, relieved as his bladder emptied.

"Make sure you don't drip on your pants, darling!" the woman yelled from the car, where she was getting some bags off the back seat.

As the boy was finishing off, another woman walked past the sidewalk, a little chubby girl almost hanging from her arm.

"Look, mummy, I can see that boy's wee-wee!" she yelled excitedly, covering her mouth with the free hand as she giggled.

"Jill, you can't say those things!" the woman chided. "I'm sorry," she added, looking at the boy's mum. "I'm Sarah Williams, and this is my daughter, Jill. We're your neighbors from across the street," she said pointing to the house on the other side of the road.

"Nice to meet you, I'm Coral Wicks, this is my little boy, Jack, and my husband, Hank."

A tall man with round glasses peeked from behind some boxes he was downloading from the boot of the car and waved.

"Hi," both Jill and Sarah waved back.

Jack ran towards the group as he zipped his pants, and stood right in front of Jill, holding a hand out for a shake.

"I don't want to shake that stinky hand!" Jill said between more giggles, and Jack's cheeks turned red.

"Jillian Williams! Don't be rude!" her mum scolded her.

Jack hid behind his mom's leg, looking at Jill through lowered lashes.

"It's okay," Coral said, "Jack is a little shy, he could do it with a friend like Jill to show him around."

To anyone looking from the outside, the difference between the kids would have been obvious. While Jack was a scrawny boy with thin and frail legs, knobby knees, and dark eyes and hair, Jill was his opposite. She had blond curls that bounced as she moved, and her limbs were chubby and rounded, her hips wide and her eyes bright green. While her skin was golden by the sun, Jack was as white as he could be. The two kids were nothing alike on the outside, and they were opposites on the inside too. Jack, on one hand, was shy and unsure of himself, dressed in mostly white or black clothing, and enjoyed flipping through pages of comics and cartoon books. On the other hand, Jill was ruthless and loud, always the center of attention. She had never cared one bit about what people thought about her and bounced around life in pink fluffy skirts and colorful tops.

Through the next few months, they became the odd pair in the neighborhood, going together everywhere as Jill showed him around and took him to the park in the corner almost every other day.

"Hello, Mrs. Wicks," Jill would always say as she knocked on the door, "can I please steal Jack?"

"Of course, are you going to the park again?"

"Yes, my mum is there with a friend, she'll look after us."

"Okay, let me go look for him."

Coral climbed the steps two at a time until she was halfway up, and called Jack's name. A few seconds later, he poked his head out of his room, a comic book between his small hands.

"What?"

"Jill is here, she wants you to go to the park with her."

"But, Mum… I want to finish this comic." Jack was barely able to read the words, but he loved them nonetheless. The stories were full of superheroes that could do everything they wanted, and he admired them for that.

"Jack, you can't be in your room all day. You'll start primary school soon, so why don't you go make some friends? A lot of the kids from the neighborhood will be attending school with you, and Jill knows them. She could introduce you to some of them."

Begrudgingly, Jack left his comic on the bedside table and walked down the stairs.

"Make sure you don't cross the road without an adult!" Coral yelled after them as the two kids trotted down the street towards the park in the corner.

The neighborhood was quiet, and not many cars drove around as they were almost to the end of a road without an exit, but still, Coral was always nervous that the kids would try to cross the road unsupervised and get hurt. So she watched them from the window, just in case.

"This is Jack, the new kid that lives down the road," Jill said as he introduced him to the other kids at the park. "He doesn't talk a lot, but he's okay. He's my friend, so he is your friend now too," she stated, very matter-of-fact.

The other kids on the park nodded, too used to Jill's antiques by then. The chubby girl grabbed Jack by his tiny wrist, and walked him around the park, dragging him behind her everywhere she went.

They played hide and seek, pretended to be superheroes, and raced down the slides all afternoon. Once, when Jill was distracted, Jack hid behind a tree, sitting down on the ground with his back against it and his legs stretched, trying to enjoy some peace and quiet. The kids were all loud, and Jack wasn't used to being surrounded by so many people at the same time.

Jill found him after a minute, and she rushed towards him, leaning into her knees as she looked down.

"What are you doing here, toothpick legs?" she nudged his knee with the tip of her boot.

Jack shrugged, and Jill laughed, launching herself towards him. She sat sideways on his lap, hugging her arms around his neck. Jack tensed, his eyes opened up wide.

"You know, you are my best friend now!" Jill stated enthusiastically.

A few weeks later, Jill and Jack started primary school together, where they made a few friends, got some decent grades, and mostly spent every second of every day together. As years went by, Jill and Jack became a known pair. They walked together to school, sat side by side in class, and hung out afterward, enjoying time in the treehouse that Hank had built for them, or running over to the park.

When they started secondary school, their mothers made sure to keep them together. They walked out of their houses at the same time and stood in the corner together as they waited for the school bus. They rode together, sitting side by side, and looked around at all the other new kids they had to get used to.

They made a few new friends, kept some of the old, and through it all, they stuck by each other's side. Halloween became their favorite time of year, where Jack could dress up as his favorite superheroes, and Jill could be her extravagant self without drawing unwanted attention.

When high school came around, Jill was there when Jack got beaten up for the first time and jumped to defend him in a second, getting a black eye and a suspension in the process. When Jill got bullied because of her looks, Jack was there to sit by her side and eat lollies with her, telling her that everything was going to be alright.

They went to the movies together, had their first illegal beer, and snuck into a pub, which they were kicked out within two minutes of arriving. Jack grew in height, but he remained as skinny as he ever was. By the time they finished junior year, he was over 6 feet tall and still had his characteristic toothpick legs. Jill was a head shorter than he was, and more than double his width. They graduated junior year being the best friends that anyone could dream of having, but they didn't know, things were about to change. A chain of events was about to start that summer between junior and senior year, and it would change the dynamics between them, even if they thought that'd be impossible.

A week into summer recess, Jack was riding his bike to the store when he got hit by a car that didn't look before turning a corner. It wasn't serious, but he spent a few days in the hospital on observation for a possible head concussion. Upon returning home, his mother decided to go spend the summer with her parents in the countryside as she claimed the family needed a break from the city.

"But Jack, what am I going to do stuck here all summer by myself?" Jill complained as he crossed the street to say goodbye a few days after the decision was made.

"I don't know! I don't want to go, but Mum is freaking out, and she wants some peace out in the fields. Grandad already said he's going to have me working all day! Do you think I want to go? I'll have to be up at five am shoving horse poo around," he complained.

"Then, stay! You can stay at my place."

"You know I can't," Jack grumbled.

"Well, this sucks!" Jill crossed her arms over her prominent chest, and Jack looked to the side, feeling guilty that he had stared at her cleavage for a second.

"Jack, time to go!" Coral yelled from across the street.

"Mrs. Wicks," Jill yelled at the top of her lungs, "this sucks di—"

"Jill!" Jack covered her mouth with his hand as his mother opened up her eyes wide, and Jill stuck her tongue out, licking his palm. "Ew!"

"Make sure you text me every damn day," Jill said as Jack wiped his hand on his jeans.

"I'll try, reception will be terrible out there."

She squeezed him into a tight hug, and Jack thought his ribs were going to crack. When she let go, she ruffled his hair and planted a loud kiss on his cheek.

"See you in September, bones," she called as he walked across the road and into the car.

It was only a few months, and even if they'd never been apart for that long, they knew their friendship would hold. After all, they were Jill and Jack, and they were like their favorite superheroes: Strongman and Magicgirl, or Cyclone and Tornado. They were their own dynamic pair—and there was nothing that could break them apart.

ELIZABETH BIGGUM

Right?

CHAPTER 2

When Jill saw the car parking in front of 252 Sunny Lane, she jumped to her feet and ran out of her room, barefoot as she was. She was wearing an over-the-knee skirt with a long-sleeved crop top, and her hair was up in a messy bun fastened with a silk scarf. She had gotten bangs a few weeks back and was wearing a pair of thick-framed sunglasses. She glanced into the mirror by the door before running out, taking in the whole 300 pounds of flesh in front of her, and smiling before fixing her skirt and opening up the front door.

As her best friend jumped off the back seat, she stopped in her tracks though. Jack had grown another few inches, but that wasn't all. His chest had filled up, his T-shirt seeming a size too small as the sleeves were filled by his biceps. His legs were still skinny but were more defined than they'd been when he left, and he was tanned, his skin almost as dark as Jill's. His hair was shorter, and it made him look older. There was a mysterious air about him, and he almost looked like the bad boy from a movie.

"Skinny bones?" Jill asked from her spot across the road.

"Jill!" Jack turned to her, a huge smile on his face.

He crossed the road and stopped in front of her, looking her up and down, "Wow, change of image?" he said, a little out of breath.

Jill had left behind her alternative looks and big fluffy skirts and was dressed in what most would have considered the latest trend. She had gotten this sudden interest in fashion during the break and had been secretly buying magazines and researching plus-size models and modeling companies in town. She was never going to admit that out loud to Jack, so she simply shrugged. It was his fault, after all, he had left her alone and she'd been so bored she'd had to find herself a new hobby.

"Could say the same for you, you've grown boobs," she joked, punching him on the chest.

"You would never believe what getting up at 5 in the morning every day and lifting sacks of manure for hours without end can do to you," he joked.

But she could, because she was seeing it first hand. She fixed her skirt again, feeling a little insecure all of a sudden.

"Are you ready to start school next Monday? I expected you to come back with a little more time to plan everything," she said, trying to divert the conversation from their looks.

"I need to head into town to buy some clothes and a new pack, actually. Would you like to come with me?"

"Sure thing! Let me get some shoes while you unload the car, and I'll meet you at the bus stop in… forty minutes?"

"Sounds great."

Coral and Hank waved from the front porch then, huge smiles on their faces. "Hi, Jill!"

"Hi, Mr. and Mrs. Wicks! It's good to have you back!"

As Jack walked back into the house, he rubbed his eyes, trying to clear his head. It'd been a while since he'd seen his best friend, but nothing had changed, right? She was still the same bubbly, silly, weird-as friend he'd always had. Why did he feel nervous being around her, then? She was just showing a bit more skin than she usually did, that was all. As he got ready to meet her back at the bus stop, he told himself he was being stupid. Nothing had changed, and he needed to keep being his usual self. He hadn't changed either, had he?

Jill swayed her hips to the music sounding on the mall as they window shopped, looking for the perfect style. Heads turned her way as she walked past, but she was oblivious to all of it, too excited to finally have her best friend back in town to notice.

"You need to tell me everything about the farm," she said, looping her arm around Jack's and bumping his side.

"She shouldn't be wearing a crop top," a girl said under her breath, giggling with her friend as she walked past them. Jack looked down, his cheeks flushing, but Jill didn't seem to hear.

"Aren't you cold? The aircon is really high," he said instead, looking at her exposed tummy.

"You know I'm never cold," she chided, shoving him to the side again, and almost making him run into a column. He laughed, shaking his head and huffing in faked-annoyance.

"Let's go in there," he said, pointing to a shop, "That's where I shop with my mum."

"Exactly why we're not going in there! We're starting senior year, it's time you stop dressing with what your mum buys you! Come on, I know a shop you'll love."

Jill took him over to a shop that had printed T-shirts with all his favorite characters from movies, tv shows, and cartoons. His eyes opened up wide when he saw the amazing selection, and he started to look over the prints, picking a few and moving them aside.

"Here," Jill tossed a shirt his way, and it landed on his head. It was a blue top with his favorite superhero's logo on it, and Jack laughed when he saw Jill holding a woman's crop top with the same logo in front of her. "I don't think they have my size, so I'm not gonna be able to match you, but you'll make a sweet hero with those new pecs!" she joked.

Jill moved to the back of the store, looking at the dresses and shaking her head every time she picked up things that said *one size fits all*. As a bunch of skinny girls walked into the store, they eyed her and started talking in whispers, giggling under their covered mouths. Jack felt his cheeks turning pink, and went to the register, ready to pay and get out of there.

As he got the bag and signaled for Jill to get out of the shop, he heard one of the girls talking to her friends.

"How come the uglies always get the hot guys?"

He pretended not to hear, but the words followed him as they walked out of the shop and Jill talked by his side, an arm looped around his shoulders. Not hearing a single word of what Jill was saying, he kept thinking about the girls in the store until it finally dawned on him, they had called him hot.

"Jill," he blurted, "Am I what girls consider a hot guy?"

Jill snorted, shaking her head as she laughed. "What the fuck are you talking about, toothpick legs? Since when do you care about what girls think?"

Jack scratched the back of his head, thinking.

"Since… always? The fact that I'm not open about it, doesn't mean I don't think about it. I know we've always been the odd ones, the freaks from school, but… has that changed?" he wondered out loud.

Jill looked him up and down, biting her bottom lip. "You'll always be a weirdo, Jack, but someone ought to find you hot, you know," she smacked him on the back of the head and kept on walking.

"I'm serious Jill! It's our senior year, if I don't get laid this year, I will probably die a virgin."

Jill snorted again, her laugh filling up the whole mall and making people turn their way. "Can't believe how much you've grown from that little kid that wouldn't say two words to me," she choked out between giggles.

Jack had always been the odd kid, and he'd been extremely shy when he was little, but a few years by Jill's side had changed that. Even if he wasn't the most popular kid in the bunch, he had learned how to speak his mind, especially in front of Jill, who never judged him for anything he said. He knew he could tell her anything, and she'd support him no matter what.

"Come on, let's get out of here," he blurted, tired of the looks they were getting from people all around them as Jill kept laughing loudly.

"Last first day of school!" Jill chanted as they walked in through the double doors and into the main hallway.

The place was already buzzing with people, and they walked together down to their usual spot between rooms A02 and A03 where an empty stretch of wall featured a couple of boys and a girl leaning against each other, already giggling and chatting along.

"Jill and Jack, good to see you!" one of their friends greeted them.

"Justin," Jill said, clapping him in the shoulder.

Justin was as short as Jill was, barely over five feet tall, and was built like a twelve-year-old kid. He had a small frame, blond hair, and light blue eyes that hid behind a pair of round glasses.

"How were your holidays?" a tall girl with pink hair asked. "Seems like you both got a glow up this recess," she added with a wink.

"It was okay," Jill replied for them, ignoring the glow-up comment with a wave of her hand, "Stick-bones here was gone for most of it, so a little boring for me," she added with a noncommittal shrug.

"Oh, hey Jack," the girl said, her dark eyes opening up a little wider.

"Penelope, nice to see you again," Jack replied with a shy smile.

"You certainly look... different," she said, unsure of which words to pick.

"He's tanned! Isn't he? Coral made him spend the summer on the farm with his grandad, and he was lifting bags of horse shit all summer long," Jill replied for him.

"No biggie," Jack said, looking down embarrassed.

"No, it looks good on you!" Penelope added quickly.

The third boy was still perched against the wall, keeping quiet as he usually did. He had opal black hair that he let grow long enough to almost cover his eyes, and was dressed fully in black, his dark brown eyes lined with kohl.

Jill went to stand next to him, and she nudged him with a shoulder.

"Ronan," she almost whispered. "Good to see you again," she smiled down at him, and the guy nodded, one side of his lips barely turning up before he looked back to the floor.

"So," Jill said back in her usual loud tone for everyone to hear, "are we ready to smash our last year of school?"

Before anyone could reply, a loud turmoil came from the door, and a group of seniors marching down the hall towards them caught their attention.

"Perfect," Ronan muttered low enough that only Jill heard him.

The group was chanting and screaming, all the most popular boys and girls that would graduate that year making a show to let the whole school know they were the ones in charge.

"Typical," Jill grunted.

The small group of friends plastered themselves against the wall not to be trampled by the jocks, and Jack tensed as the group got closer. For years on end, the small group of friends had been the target for the jocks' jokes. They had been pushed around, bullied, name-called, it was never violent, but it wasn't fun either. Jack knew that year wouldn't be different, but something inside of him wished to be invisible, for that day to be the exception.

As expected, one of them addressed him as they passed, "Hey, bones," he said, punching him in the shoulder a little too hard.

"Don't tease him!" Jill jumped straight away.

"Why not?"

"He's mine, so back off," Jill snapped, pushing the guy back.

His friends caught him, and all of them laughed out loud looking at the pair of them.

"Sticks here still needs a bodyguard," they laughed.

A blonde girl with a cheerleader uniform approached, looking at them all up and down.

"I think that nickname doesn't suit Jack anymore," she said softly, setting a hand over Jack's biceps.

Without another word, the girl turned around with a swipe of her hair and kept on walking. The jocks looked at her with their mouths hanging open like fishes out of water. As the final bell rang, they all scattered quickly. All except Jill and Jack, who stood on the spot.

"Did Gwendoline just touch my bicep?" Jack whispered in a trance.

Jill smacked him in the head and then pointed to the hall. "Come on, let's go, we're gonna be late, Sticks."

Jack followed along, but his mind was far gone. *Had one of the most popular girls in school jumped up to defend him? And she'd known his name!*

CHAPTER 3

The first few weeks of school passed in a blur. Nothing was too different than it used to be, but there was a weird vibe in the air that everyone kept picking up on. The small group of friends hung out as usual, but the jocks were now keeping a little distance, not bothering them as much.

During lunchtime, Gwendoline started glancing at Jack, and Jack couldn't get his eyes off the beautiful cheerleader. Gwen was the girl every boy in school dreamt about: tall, long legs, shiny blond hair, and blue eyes that always seemed to be judging you but you couldn't help but stare into. She was beautiful, and she knew it and used it to her advantage on the daily. And Jack had her attention, and he didn't know why, but he knew he'd be an idiot to pass the opportunity. Rumor had it that Gwendoline had been dating a college guy during summer, but the relationship had ended up badly, so she was single again. *Maybe she was looking for a rebound guy.*

"Jack, Earth calling to Jack."

He looked at Jill, who was staring at him with a hard look on her face.

"What?" he asked.

"What in hell is wrong with you? You've been an idiot for the last few days, you're in a damn cloud, worse than usual. I've been talking to you for like ten minutes!"

"Sorry, I was daydreaming," he shrugged, trying to dismiss the issue.

"Come on, we're leaving," she pulled him up from his T-shirt, lifting him with ease as if he didn't weigh at all.

"Sure, sure," Jack grabbed his backpack, glancing back at Gwendoline's spot once more before walking away. When he looked though, the blond girl was gone and her seat was empty. *Weird,* he thought.

They made it to the doors, and as they were stepping into the hallway, a hand wrapped around Jack's wrist, making him jump up.

"Jack," Gwendoline said softly, her cold fingers making shivers run up his arm. "I was wondering if you'd walk with me to my next class, I have a lot of books to carry for a project, and I don't have enough hands to do so myself."

Jack looked at her with wide eyes, opening and closing his mouth without finding any words. "Hmm, uhm, yeah," he mumbled after a minute.

Jack drifted from his group, not noticing the evil stare as Jill glared his way when he retreated. Gwendoline made small talk, asking Jack about his assignments and classes while he mumbled a few answers and she led him to her locker. She got a whole heap of books out, handing them out to him one by one until he was holding a pile so high it was almost about to topple.

Gwendoline closed the locker and grabbed the two books from the top of the pile, leaving Jack to carry the rest.

"Thank you for helping me," she said with a wicked smile that made him wonder what was going on.

As weeks went by, Gwendoline kept finding excuses to run into Jack, and Jack kept finding excuses to be in the same place as her as often as possible. They made small talk, and Jack was still too insecure to ask her out, but he knew the time was coming. He needed to do it. If he wanted to lose his virginity before the end of the year, he'd have to make a move sooner or later. And what better than having Gwendoline be the girl to do it with?

It was a week before Halloween when Jill knocked on his door in the afternoon. Coral let her in, and without asking for permission, she made her way upstairs to Jack's room. Jack was not allowed to have girls in his room, but Jill had always been the exception.

"Hey, asshole, what are you up to?"

Jill dropped herself onto Jack's bed and looked at him as he typed on his computer by the desk.

"Hey, Jill," he said half-heartedly, his eyes on the screen.

Jill waited a moment, and when Jack didn't say anything else, she broke the silence again.

"I was thinking about the Halloween party…"

That picked Jack's interest, and he stopped typing, turning the chair around in a circle and looking at her with eager eyes.

"Yes!" he chanted. "I've been thinking about that too," he leaned forward and glanced at the door quickly before looking back at her.

Jill sat up and faced him, wondering what the fuss was about. As every year, there was a party that their class organized, and they always went together. They hadn't had time to organize their costumes that year due to assignments, but that was why Jill was visiting, she'd had an amazing idea for them to get matching costumes that she was sure Jack would love.

"So," Jack said, gathering up the courage to say what he wanted to say. "I've been thinking about asking Gwendoline to go to the party with me," he said it all in one breath, talking as fast as he could.

Jill looked at him with her mouth hanging open and snapped it close when she realized what she was doing.

"Great, just do it then," she snapped.

"Well, yes, but I… you know, have never done anything like it, so I was wondering if you could help me?"

"Help you how?" Jill raised an eyebrow, her arms crossed over her chest.

"I don't know!" he complained, lifting his arms in the air to show his annoyance. "But you're a girl, maybe you could tell me how I'm meant to do this or something. I never talk with girls, I don't know how to."

Jill's face was an unreadable mask as she stared at him.

"I don't know if you'd noticed," she said in a clipped tone, "but I'm not the kind of girl that gets invited to parties. And you talk with me every single day."

With that, she got up and stormed out of the room, her steps resonating on the walls as she raced down the stairs and slammed the door behind her.

Jack was left staring at the door, wondering what could have upset her so much. In the long years they'd been friends, they had never had a real fight. They'd argued all the time, and Jill had always called him names, and they'd play-fight often, but they had never really fought about anything. So Jack shook his head, thinking she was probably moody because of her period again, and went back to his homework, typing away as he thought about how he could bring up the Halloween party in a conversation with Gwendoline.

To his surprise, he didn't even need to try. He was at school the next day when Gwen walked past him and stopped by his side.

"Hi, Jack," she said, brushing her hair behind her ear.

"Oh, Gwen, I was just... going to go looking for you," he stammered.

"Where you?" she replied in a sweet tone.

"Yes, I was thinking, you know how there's the —ehm, party, next week... I was wondering, if maybe—"

"Oh, the Halloween party!" Gwendoline interrupted, "I'd almost forgotten about it! Would you like to pick me up for it? That would be great of you, and we could go together. My car is going to be in the mechanic that weekend, so I need the ride."

Jack's jaw slacked, and he nodded, unable to form any words.

"Perfect, see you around Jack."

As she walked away, Jack looked at Jill with wide eyes. "Can you believe that? I'm going to a party with Gwen! Cheerleader Gwen!" he said excitedly.

Jill rolled her eyes and clapped him in the shoulder without humor. "Congratulations, Champ," she said without emotion before walking away.

Jack was too excited to notice Jill's disappointment, and went on with his day on light feet, telling everybody that would listen that he had a date with Gwendoline.

Halloween came and went in the blink of an eye, the day too full of excitement for Jack to notice what was going on until the day was almost over. He'd gone to the party with Gwen, had a few too many drinks, danced, laughed at his own jokes, and kissed her. *He'd kissed Gwendoline Miller.* Jack Wicks had kissed Gwendoline Miller. He still couldn't believe it. Before the night was over, Gwen had kissed him. It had been brief, and almost cute, but it had happened, and they'd been texting during the whole weekend afterward.

When Jack jumped off the bus on Monday morning, he went

straight to the spot where he knew he'd find Gwen, briefly telling Jill that he'd see her after class as there was something he wanted to do.

He was nervous as he approached her, but needed to make sure what had happened on the weekend was real, and that he hadn't dreamed it. Imagine his surprise as he got near her, and Gwendoline turned around, smiling up at him and engulfing him in a quick hug.

"Hey, Jack," she said.

"Hi," he replied, and as soon as the word was out of his mouth, Gwen swallowed it with a kiss.

It was real. It was happening, and Gwen was kissing him on the school grounds. *What did that mean? Were they together? Did that mean they were a couple now? A real thing?* Jack was so inexpert in the matters of the heart, that he wasn't sure if he was meant to ask all those questions or not.

As he walked her over to her class and left her at the door, he wondered tentatively, "Should I come to get you at the bell?"

"Of course," Gwen said. "We go everywhere together now," she added with a wink.

That's how Gwendoline and Jack became the new subject everyone at school was talking about. The most popular girl from school was dating ex-freak Jack, who was now considered one of the top five hottest guys in senior year. His jump on the social scale meant new friends, as Gwendoline's friends became his friends too, and Jack started to spend lunch hour at the same table as the jocks that had teased him so many times before.

In a few days, he became friends with Chad, Riley, and Kayle, spending all his afternoons with them and riding at the back of the bus as well.

Jill was still there, and they talked in the halls and classes that they shared, but she became distant, something that Jack barely noticed with his newly-found popularity. He was living the dream, having the life every guy his age wanted to have, and he got lost in the emotions, turning away from who he used to be.

"I haven't seen Jill around in a couple of weeks," Coral told him one afternoon. "Is everything okay between the two of you?"

They had just finished dinner, and Hank was doing the dishes in the kitchen while Coral and Jack finished picking everything from the table.

"Of course, why wouldn't it?" Jack retorted.

"I don't know, you tell me. You haven't mentioned her in a while either."

"I don't know, I guess we're both busy. You know, last year of school, college applications to think about, new friends, girl-friend…"

He let the word hang in the air, and Coral looked at him for a moment before recognition showed in her face.

"Girlfriend? You have a girlfriend?" she asked, a big smile on her face now.

"Yeah, I do. Her name is Gwendoline. She's pretty cute, I think you'd like her."

Coral hugged him, and then pulled out two chairs, signaling for him to take a seat and sitting in front of him, her curious eyes shining bright.

"You need to tell me more about her," Coral said. "What's she going to study in college, what are her plans?"

"I… I don't know," Jack admitted, having no clue of the answer.

"Oh, okay, I guess there's time to talk about those things. Well, what does she do? What hobbies does she have?"

"Well, she's in the cheerleading squad…"

"A cheerleader? You'll have to find me a picture of her."

"Mum, don't be pushy!" Jack complained, getting up from the chair and picking the remaining plates to take them to the kitchen.

"Oh, come on, I want to know more!"

Jack laughed and ignored the questions, not because he didn't want to tell his mum about Gwen, but because he realized he didn't know the answer to pretty much any of those questions.

CHAPTER 4

Senior year is one of the key moments in the life of any teen, and still, time seems to go by so fast, that when you realize, you're halfway through the year and still have no clue on what you're supposed to be doing with your life. This was no different for Jill and Jack. While they still sat together at lunch every other day and waited for the bus side by side, there seemed to be a gap in between them that they didn't know how to close.

Jack and Gwendoline's relationship wasn't the talk of the town anymore, but it was certainly the only thing Jack could think about. Or so he told himself, as he desperately ignored the thoughts in the back of his mind.

"Should we go bowling this weekend?" Jack asked Gwendoline one afternoon in mid-March.

They had been dating for almost four months, but all their activities seemed to be group ones, and they never really spent that much time together being alone. Jack needed to change that. If his plan was to work, he needed more time alone with Gwendoline to start getting intimate. They had kissed in public several times, but that had been about it.

"Bowling? Sounds a little lame, why don't we go to the movies?" she offered instead.

Jack kept his expression cool, but couldn't help but relive the memories. He used to go bowling with Jill all the time, and he used to have so much fun doing it! It had been one of their favorite activities since they were kids, but that was okay —movies were fun too.

"Movies will do, I'll pick you up at seven on Saturday, okay?"

Jack picked Gwendoline up as arranged and they drove together to the mall. The movie theater was on the top floor, and they made their way up there while making small talk. Jack could feel eyes turning their way, and felt a little self-conscious about it. Gwen was wearing a mini skirt that showed off her long legs, and a long-sleeved crop top. The weather was becoming warmer again, but it wasn't that warm yet.

"Aren't you cold?" Jack asked, memories from another mall trip making their way into his head.

"A little, but it's okay."

"Do you want my jacket?" he offered, thinking it'd be the right thing to say.

"No, it's okay, it won't match what I'm wearing."

Silence stretched again as they made their way to the clerk and Jack paid for two tickets.

The movie was a boring romance that Gwen seemed to enjoy, but Jack found it excruciating slow. Whenever he went to the movies with Jill, they watched either action movies or thrillers, which always had them at the edge of their seats with excitement. Jack shook his head, trying to get the memories out of his head. He was with Gwen, and that was a good thing. They'd held hands during parts of the movie, and he had even been brave enough to get his arms around her for the last half of the movie. By the end of it, his arm was numb and tingly, and Jack was feeling tired and frustrated —as well as hungry.

"Should we grab something to eat?" he wondered as soon as they were out of the room.

"Okay, I guess I could eat something," Gwen replied with a shrug.

They made their way to the cafeteria, and Jack ordered a triple burger with fries and a large coke. Despite his size, Jack ate a lot. He could eat as much as he wanted and never really gain any weight, something which Jill had always scolded him for.

"You're so damn lucky," she always said.

But she didn't mind the fact that it didn't apply to her, and still, she always ordered a small burger with a side of fries whenever they went to the movies. She ate a healthy diet but didn't deprive herself of enjoying something delicious whenever they went out.

"I'll have the salad," Gwen said when they ordered, and Jack couldn't help but feel disappointed for some reason.

By the time spring came around, Jack was still stuck on first base and had no clue why his relationship wasn't progressing any further. He liked Gwen, she was good-looking and made time for him, but something was missing, and he couldn't figure out what it was. He was hanging out with her one particularly hot Friday when Chad came over and interrupted them.

"Hey, lads!" he said as a way of greeting.

"Hey, Chad," he replied, clapping him on the back. "What's up?"

"We're welcoming this hot wave with a bang, and I'm here to invite you to an epic day at the beach! The more the merrier, so please invite anyone you know, we're taking over South Beach. Do you know where the Shack is?"

"The shack?" Jack asked, confused.

"It's an old wooden thing we put up last summer, if it's still standing. It's on a pretty private stretch of beach we found after a small walk through the bush."

"I know where it is," Gwen cut in, "I'll show him the way."

"Perfect! And remember, invite as many people as you can!"

Jack instantly thought of Jill. They hadn't spoken in weeks, it seemed like he hadn't even seen her around lately, and he felt like he finally had an excuse to go over to her. After school, he decided, he'll knock on her door and invite her.

The day was over faster than expected, and Gwen offered Jack a ride home. Jack looked around the parking lot, trying to spot Jill, but when he didn't see her, he accepted Gwen's offer.

"I'll pick you up tomorrow," Gwen said, saying goodbye with a quick kiss when she dropped him off.

As soon as Gwendoline's car rounded the corner, Jack crossed the street and knocked on Jill's door. He heard steps on the other side, and after a moment, Jill opened the door. Her expression was closed off as she looked at him, but a small smile took over her face after a minute of awkward silence.

"What are you doing here, Bones?"

"I thought I owed you a visit," Jack replied, not sure of what to say.

"Is your girlfriend too busy today?" she retorted while lifting her brows.

"I'm—I... I'm so sorry."

Jack looked down to the tips of his shoes, not knowing what to say or how to act. Jill was staring at him, and he could feel her eyes on him, which made his stomach churn and his insides feel warm. *What was wrong with him?*

"What are you sorry for? For getting a girlfriend and forgetting I even exist?"

Jill's tone was collected, like she didn't mind that Jack had been out of her life, and for some reason, that made it even worse. No matter how hard he tried to look away, Jill was so short that looking down wasn't making him any favors, so he gave up, looking straight into her bright green eyes.

"Yes, exactly what you said," Jack agreed. "I've been an ass, and you deserve better."

Jill looked surprised and laughed out loud as she reached up and punched Jack on the chest, "You are an ass," she admitted with a chuckle. "So, why are you here?"

"I wanted to invite you to an outing tomorrow. We're going to the beach to celebrate the start of the summer, and I was told I could invite my friends," Jack admitted.

"And now you remember that we're still friends," Jill mumbled, but then she smiled, shaking her head as if to get rid of that comment. "Okay," she said. "Okay, that's... that's fine, I'll go to the beach with you and your friends."

Jack found himself smiling from ear to ear, the idea of spending time with Jill again after so long making him happy in a way he forgot he could be.

"Gwen is picking me up, do you want to catch a ride with us?"

Jill seemed to think about it for a second, and then shook her head, "No, it's okay, send me your geo-location when you get there and I'll find my way."

"Okay."

"Okay..."

They stood there, looking at each other for another minute until Jill pushed him back into the street.

"I got shit to do, see you tomorrow, Jack," she said, closing the door between them.

Jack stood there for a moment before crossing the street, feeling out of place. He couldn't remember the last time Jill had used his name instead of some kind of insult or nickname, and he felt unsettled by it. *Had things changed that much between them?*

Jack was lying on his back, a can of beer in one hand, and a cigarette in the other. He was used to drinking a beer here and there, but it was the first time he was having a smoke. Chad had offered it to him, and not knowing how to say no, he had accepted it. The thing was just hanging awkwardly from his fingers, and he made a huge effort to keep talking and pretend to be busy not to take another drag any time soon. The first one had almost cost him a coughing fit, and he hadn't looked as smug as he intended to.

Gwen was a few feet away, taking selfies by the water while only dipping her feet. She was wearing a small bikini that showed every small curve of her body and as much skin as Jack had ever seen. The yellow color of the fabric brought up her tan a notch, making her skin seem even darker than it was. Jack had no doubt her tan was fake, but he didn't mind it.

"Damn, you're lucky, Wicks," Chad joked, punching him on the shoulder. "I wish I was the one sleeping around with that beauty."

"Damn straight! The things I'd do to her!" Riley added, taking another sip of his beer and looking across the beach with hungry eyes.

Jack laughed uncomfortably, nodding his head in agreement. He couldn't tell them nothing had happened between them, but he wasn't about to admit out loud to something that wasn't true either.

"I bet she's amazing in bed," Chad nudged him in the shoulder again, and Jack looked at him blankly. "Come on, don't be shy, we're in confidence here!"

Jack opened his mouth to say something—anything—but was silenced by Kyle's next comment.

"Oh. My. Lord. Would you look at that? The beach is at full capacity now," he said, pointing with his head somewhere behind Jack.

They were half under the place the guys had called 'the shack', which had turned out to be more like a barely standing pile of sticks. It was like a teepee without the canvas on top. Jack turned around, poking his head past the post next to him, and his cigarette fell into the sand as he took in the sight in front of him. Jill had her hair half pinned up, with loose curls framing her face, and her fringe perfectly in line. She was wearing a white summer dress with bright yellow sunflowers. It had a low neckline, and Jack's mouth hung open as he stared. He closed it quickly, returning his attention to his friends. They had been talking all the while, but he wasn't sure what they'd say.

He stood up, excused himself, and shook some sand off his legs before making his way towards her.

"Hey, Jill. Uhm, glad you could make it. Found your way here okay?"

"It was fine, a few mosquito bites on the walk here, but nothing terrible," she said, panting a little.

"The walk can be tiring, wanna sit with us?" he said, pointing to the boys lying down close by.

They all waved, and Jack heard them laughing and talking among themselves again.

"I think I might go for a dip first if that's okay, I'm feeling pretty damn hot after that walk," she complained, wiping invisible sweat off her forehead and pinning her fringe back with a clip she got from her pocket.

"Yeah, sure thing, just… join us when you're done?"

At the same time as Jill walked towards the water, Gwen was coming back. Jack walked back to his spot, being distracted as his eyes kept sweeping back to Jill. She had stopped a few feet away from the water and was leaving her bag and belongings on a dead tree trunk.

"Want another drink, Jack?" Gwen asked as he sat next to him.

He nodded and grabbed the can she was offering as he lowered himself to the sand.

The conversation around him resumed, and he replied with 'um's and 'yeah's while his eyes kept darting back and forth from the water. The place started to fill up with more people, someone put on some loud music, and more drinks and smokes started to go around them. Jill was in the water, splashing around in a high-waisted two-piece swimsuit that didn't leave much to the imagination. It was the same shade of green as her eyes, and for some strange reason, Jack couldn't stop looking. In the twelve years he had known her, he had never seen her in a bikini before.

She returned from the water a long while later and sat at the corner of the group, a few people away from Jack. Gwen was now sitting on his lap, so he couldn't move much, but he turned his body towards her and gave her one small smile before returning to the conversation with his friends. She was wrapped up in a towel, and when a breeze picked up and she shivered, Jack bit the inside of his cheek.

"I better go get my stuff," she muttered when the sun started going down and the temperature dropped another few degrees. She walked away, and a few eyes followed her as she did.

"I don't know how she does that," Gwen said.

"Do what?" Jack asked dumbly.

"Walk around in a bikini without shame," she replied. Jack's breathing stilled.

"She belongs to the sea," Chad laughed a drunk kind of laughter, "she's a whale, get it?"

Jack felt his cheeks burning up and bit his tongue. He couldn't see her from where he was as his back was to the water, so he took a big swing at his beer, emptying half the can in one go as his friends kept laughing. His head spun, and he swallowed hard.

"At least she's got boobs," Kayle said, "you could get lost in there," he added with a laugh of his own.

"Wicks," Chad punched him in the shoulder as he usually did to get his attention, "didn't you two used to date? How's getting your face lost in there?"

The whole group cracked up laughing at that, and Jack felt his neck burning hotter and hotter.

"I— We... never dated," he stammered. As the whole group kept laughing, he blurted out the worst thing he'd ever said, "I—I could never date such a... blob."

He regretted the words the moment they were out of his mouth, and he bit his tongue as hard as he could without making it bleed. The whole group cracked with another round of laughter, and he suddenly felt like he was being watched. He turned his head back just in time to see a white and yellow blurred image running out into the entrance to the passage that led back to the parking lot. *Jill?*

"I'll be right back," he told Gwen as he pushed her off his lap and got up.

"Where are you going?" She grabbed his wrist, pulling him closer to her.

"I need to go take a leak," he replied quickly as he looked back into the place where Jill had disappeared.

"Okay, don't take too long," she kissed him on the lips before letting go of his hand, and Jack started towards the path, walking as fast as he could without running.

The sun was completely down by then, and the beach was getting dark. Someone had started a bonfire closer to the water, but as soon as he stepped into the path, it was almost black. He saw a white light far in the distance between the bushes as if someone was illuminating the path with a torch or a phone, and he wished he'd been smart enough to grab his own.

It took him a while to get back to the lot, and once he did, he saw the light inside Sarah William's car. He didn't know when Jill had started driving it, and that on its own made a pang of guilt burn upon his chest. He started for the car and stopped dead on his feet as he saw Jill wiping tears from her eyes and fixing the rearview mirror. In twelve years, Jack hadn't seen Jill cry, not once. Not even when her cat had died when she'd been twelve. Not when she had been bullied over and over at school. Not when a kid had given her a black eye for defending him. *Not once.*

He was bolted to the spot as the engine raved and Jill backed the car quickly and got out of the lot without even noticing him standing in the darkness.

He was an asshole.

CHAPTER 5

Jack had stumbled back to the beach and tried —fruitlessly— to convince Gwen to go back home. After a few more hours, in which he had sobered up and not been able to have another drink, he had driven Gwen back to her house and taken a cab to his place. All the lights at Jill's house had been off by the time he returned, so he'd gone to bed with a sour feeling in his gut, unable to apologize to her.

The next morning, he had debated knocking on her door but hadn't been brave enough. Not until after lunch, when he'd finally gone across the road. Sarah had opened the door and told him that Jill wasn't at home and that she didn't know when she'd be back. He could smell the lie, but he guessed he deserved it and let it go.

He texted her. Called her. Posted on her secret blog that no one else knew about. Left a note stuck to her bedroom's window as he had done when they were kids. Called her again. Texted her some more.

Nothing.

He heard nothing of her. It was as if Jill had completely disappeared from the earth. When Monday came around, she wasn't at the bus stop in the morning either. A gut-wrenching feeling made him want to throw up at the thought that he'd fucked up worse than he'd even realized.

When the bus pulled up at school, he headed straight to the spot between rooms A02 and A03, a place he hadn't spent any time at in the last few months. He felt guilty as he slowly walked towards the small group. She was already there. They were all deep into some kind of conversation, and when he stood behind Jill, none of them looked his way.

"Jill?" he asked tentatively.

Her shoulders tensed but she didn't turn. She said something to Justin, who looked down to the floor not to make eye contact with him as he replied.

"Jill?" he tried again.

This time, Jill stopped talking mid-sentence and squared her shoulders. She looked to the side, to where Penelope was standing and hooked her arm around hers.

"Let's go to class, the halls are getting crowded," she said. And with that, both girls walked away, leaving Jack standing with his mouth hanging open.

"Justin?" he dared look at the other boy, and he looked down at his boots.

"Sorry, Jack," he said before walking away.

"Wow, what's going on? Ronan?"

There was a heavy silence before his friend looked up at him. He stared right into his eyes, and then took one deep breath, "You're an asshole," he said as he breathed out.

It was the first time Jack had ever heard a curse out of the guy's mouth, and he was rooted to the spot as Ronan also walked away, leaving him alone in the hall.

Days and weeks went by, and Jack kept being ignored by his old friends. Jill had started to drive to school, so she was never at the bus stop anymore, and he never saw her around the neighborhood either. Sometimes, he saw her driving in later in the afternoon, and he wondered what she was up to. Jill had never had many activities outside of school, and the truth was that he was curious. And jealous. And he missed her.

He tried to pretend like he didn't care. Hanging out with Gwendoline's friends, going out on dates, and to parties with his new buddies. But he never felt completely comfortable with them. It was a sunny April afternoon when Jack was sitting on his desk by the window, trying to get an assignment done while contemplating the road. Sarah's car wasn't at the entrance, but he knew Sarah was at home as he'd seen her planting some new flowers by the fence. The sun was getting close to the horizon, and the car still wasn't back. Jack's stomach twisted. By the time the car rounded the corner, the sun was halfway behind the houses in the distance, and the lights on the street were already on.

"What are you up to?" Jack wondered out loud.

The words came back to bite him as he saw Jill get out of the car. She was wearing a beautiful dress with ballerina flats, her hair had perfect curls, and even from a distance, Jack was almost sure she was wearing make-up. It was in the way her cheeks glistened under the streetlamp, and the shade of her lips, which was darker than usual. Imagine Jack's shock when the passenger's door opened and a tall guy got out. He was wearing dress pants and a shirt, his hair neat and perfect, and he had a smile that seemed to belong in a magazine. Jack leaned forward into the window, trying to catch any details, but the guy was quickly giving him his back as both of them marched into the house. Jill opened the door, letting the guy in without looking back.

Jack slumped on the bed, grabbed his phone, and texted Gwen to see if she wanted to hang out that night. He needed out of there, he needed a distraction.

Would he stay for dinner? Would he see him leave in a few hours? Or simply minutes? He didn't want to know, he wanted to be out of there not to have to worry about any of that.

To his surprise, Gwen called him.

"Hey, Gwen," he said into the phone.

"Hey, your text couldn't have come at a better time, do you want to go out somewhere? I can pick you up."

Jack thought he heard screaming in the background, and the sound of something breaking.

"Yeah, sure… Are you okay?"

"Everything's perfectly fine, I'll be at your place in ten minutes, okay?"

"Sure, I'll be ready."

Jack jumped off the bed and couldn't help looking out the window. The lights were on in the dining room as well as Jill's bedroom, and Jack had to look away. He closed the curtains and got changed quickly, putting on some cologne and brushing his teeth before grabbing his keys and jacket.

"Mum, I'm going out!" he yelled down the hall as he marched to the front door.

Hank poked his head from the kitchen, looking at him up and down. "Going out with your girl?" he asked.

"Yeah, I am. Is that okay?"

"Sure thing, just make sure to be a gentleman, and always be careful, okay?" he added with a wink.

Jack had had the birds and the bees conversation when he was eleven, and every year, Hank had made sure to add more information and reiterate what Jack already knew.

"I know, Dad," he said, almost laughing. He was so used to it by now, that he wasn't embarrassed by the conversations anymore. "Where's mum at?"

"She went out with some friends, said she wouldn't be back till late. Here I was hoping for a night of football and beers with my boy… I guess it'll be next time."

"Next time," Jack agreed as he heard a honk at the door. "I better go."

He ran out and jumped into Gwen's car as fast as he could, trying not to let his eyes go to the car parked across the street.

"Hi," he leaned forward, pressing his lips to Gwen's.

Gwen kissed him back, and when he tried to pull away, she laced her fingers in the back of his neck, bringing him back closer and kissing him deeper than she's ever had.

"Wow," Jack muttered like an idiot when she finally let go.

"Let's get out of here, I need some fresh air," Gwen said nonchalantly like she hadn't just dug her tongue into Jack's throat.

He kept glancing at Gwen as she drove. Her eyes seemed to be puffy, and she was gripping the steering wheel so tight that her knuckles were going white. She was heading the opposite way they normally went, and Jack was lost for words. *Should he ask if she was okay? What if she started crying when he did?* He wasn't sure how to act if a girl cried.

"Where are we going?" he asked instead, playing it safe.

"The mount," she replied with a shrug.

Jack swallowed hard. The mount wasn't too far, it was more like a small hill from where you could watch the city lights, and it was a known place where people went to make out. *Was it about to happen?* He suddenly wished he'd showered before leaving the house. But it was okay, he'd showered that morning. And he always had condoms in his wallet. They had been there waiting since he was fifteen, only coming out to be thrown out when the expiry dates came up, to be replaced with new ones. He'd been waiting for so long, and now there was a chance it was actually about to happen, and he wasn't sure he was ready. Feeling his palms sweating, he ran them down his jeans.

They drove in silence, and when they got to the top, Gwen parked up under a tree in the darkness. The sun was completely gone, and a few stars were visible in the sky. Jack looked at Gwen, back out the window, and then at Gwen again.

"Are—"

Before he could say another word, Gwen leaned over the shift and pressed her lips against him, silencing his questions. One of her hands was on his shoulder, and the other grabbing the back of his head, tangling in his hair. Jack reached out, looping his arms around her back and helping her as she got her legs over and landed her knees one to each side of his hips. He felt the warmth spreading through his body, the blood going down and giving him a head rush. He was high on emotions, his whole body demanding more, and more, until a familiar voice spoke in the back of his head.

"Make sure to ask for consent," Hank always said to him.

Gwen had pushed back and was kissing his neck, opening up the buttons of his shirt. His heart was racing so fast, he wasn't sure he could find his voice, but he made an effort.

"Are you sure this is okay?" he asked.

"Shut up," Gwen said, "and use your lips for something better."

There was a wicked smile on her face, and she leaned back, her hands disappearing behind her. Jack's eyes opened up wide as he realized she was unclasping her bra. She got the straps out without taking her singlet off and threw the piece of lace into the back seat. Gwen's lips were on his again in a second, and she grabbed one of his hands, guiding it to her chest. They had never gotten that far, and Jack closed his eyes, savoring every second and not being able to believe what was going on. They were a messy tangle of limbs, neither of them sure of what they were doing as they explored each other's bodies. They kept bumping into the door, and Jack couldn't stop thinking about how small and uncomfortable the car was. He did his best to get all thought out of his mind, letting it drift to better places. He closed his eyes again, thinking of the curves of the body in front of him, the feel of her mouth on his, her lips pressing into his collarbone. He thought of luscious curves, blond curls, and green eyes.

"Oh, Jill—"

The world still. The words had escaped his mouth unexpectedly, and in a second, Gwendoline had gone still. She pulled back slowly, looking at Jack with a few tears glistening in her eyes. She shook her head and then she moved so fast, Jack could barely react. She opened the door of the car and jumped out, running to the edge of the cliff and sitting on the grass, her legs to her chest and her arms around them.

Jack was stunned for a second, and then he ran after her, buttoning up his shirt and fixing his jacket as he did.

"Gwen, I'm so... I—"

The look Gwendoline gave him as she looked back silenced him. "Don't," she said simply.

Her cheeks were streaked with tears, and she was shaking. The wind had picked up, and Jack took his jacket off and put it over her shoulders. She gripped it tight as she cried, and Jack stood there, not sure of what to do.

After a few minutes, Gwen calmed down and lifted her head, looking into the horizon. "They're splitting up," she simply said.

"What?"

"My parents. They're getting a divorce."

"Oh."

Jack didn't know what to say, so he moved closer, sitting by her side and resting an arm across her shoulder gently, unsure if she was going to accept the gesture. To his surprise, Gwen leaned against his side.

"I'm so sorry," he said. "I had no idea."

"No one does. I haven't talked about it with anyone… I'm 'perfect Gwendoline', you know? I have an image people expect to see."

"Gwen, that… that's not okay," he finally said, finding his words. "You're an amazing girl, you should just be who you are. You are caring, but you try to hide that to be cool, to be liked… I think people would like you more for who you truly are."

"I'm just a pretty face, Jack. That's what I am. And even with that… you still prefer Jill," she snorted.

"I don't, I—"

Gwen pulled away and looked at him in the eyes, "You should stop lying to yourself, it's pretty obvious. I can't even be mad at you about it, because I knew. I knew from the start, and I ignored it because I thought you'd forget about her being with me."

"What do you mean, you knew?" Jack asked dumbly.

"It's in the way you look at her and talk about her. You never look at me like that," Gwen said with a shrug, like it wasn't a big thing.

Jack was lost for words, trying to process what he was hearing.

"Why were you with me then?" he asked, his head spinning with thoughts and everything Gwen had just said.

"I didn't want to be alone," she replied in a small voice. "You're a good guy, Jack. But I knew you weren't the one. I just needed someone to be there for me… I'm sorry, I know it was wrong."

"I'm sorry, too," Jack admitted. He had known Gwen wasn't the one, but he had used her for what he wanted the same way she had used him.

They stayed like that for a while, Gwen leaning against his side as silent tears rolled down her cheeks while Jack kept thinking about the last few months. About every day Jill hadn't been there, and how much it had hurt.

Eventually, Gwendoline sighed loudly and offered to take him back home. The night hadn't been what neither of them had expected, and she guessed by them, her parents would be done arguing.

"You know, you can still count on me if you ever need a friend," Jack said when Gwen left him at his place.

"I know," Gwen replied, a sad smile on her lips. "You'll be a good boyfriend to the right girl," she added as he jumped off the car.

She drove away before he could reply.

CHAPTER 6

Jack found his father on the couch when he returned, half asleep while the game was still playing in the background. He grabbed the remote, turned the volume down, and sat by his side.

"Oh, hey kiddo, you're back," his dad said, rubbing the sleep off his eyes. "How was your night?"

"It was... okay..."

That seemed to wake Hank up, and he straightened up, sitting against the armrest and facing his son.

"Okay, tell me, what's going on?"

Jack thought about what to say for a while, images of both Gwen and Jill circling his mind. He'd had a good time with Gwendoline in the past few months, but he had never felt a real connection with her. The whole time by her side, it was as if something was missing.

"How do you know if someone is the right person for you?" he finally asked.

"Oh..." Hank seemed to think it over, looking at Jack with interest. "I think it might be different for each person. But it's someone you enjoy spending time with. Someone you want to push to see them do better. Someone that lights up your day with their mere presence. Things in a relationship are never perfect, it's all about communication. You need to find someone you can talk with, that will listen and you'll be willing to listen to."

Jack was silent for a moment, taking in everything his dad had said and trying to figure out how to move forward. He'd fucked up big time with Jill, and the more he thought about it, the more he saw the signs of everything he'd felt for her and had tried to bury down deep not to damage their friendship. And now he didn't have either a girlfriend or a friend because of it.

"Dad…" he said, doubting himself for a minute. "How do you fix things when you've hurt someone's feelings?"

Hank took a deep breath, and then clasped a hand on Jack's shoulder.

"Jack, they say actions are more valued than words… but most of the time, I doubt that. You can give a woman flowers, chocolates, or whatever present you might think of, but at the end of the day, what people most value is honestly. Be honest, be open, be vulnerable. And if you made a mistake, apologize."

"Thanks, dad," it was all he could say. There was too much going on in his head, and he needed time to think it all over.

Jack went to his room and laid in bed, looking at the roof as he thought about what his dad's words. There was another thought that kept poking in his mind though… what if Jill had moved on? What if she had someone in her life and she no longer wanted him to be a part of it? After hours without being able to sleep, Jack got to a conclusion: it didn't matter if she didn't want him in her life anymore, that was no excuse. He still needed to apologize and make sure she knew he had messed up, big time.

But first, he needed to get her attention.

Jack got to school the next day with the certainty that we wouldn't get to the end of the day without talking with Jill. But when he walked in the main door, the first thing he saw was Gwendoline, standing with their friends, and he stopped for a moment, unsure of how to proceed. *Should they act as friends? Did Gwen hate him now?* They seemed to have finished on good terms the day before, but he was unsure of what to say or do. He walked towards her slowly, reading her expression. She smiled, and it was a small thing that didn't really reach her eyes. He stopped by her side, and planted a kiss on her forehead. Leaning down, he spoke in her ear.

"Are you okay?"

It didn't matter if they weren't together anymore, he cared about her, and if there was something he had learned by talking with his dad the night before, was to be true to who he was. And he wasn't the type of person to ignore someone after a break-up.

"I'm okay," she replied, looking around nervously. "I don't want to make a scene, but I don't want people to see us together either, Jack. Just… let's keep our distance for a while, okay?"

"Are you sure that's what you want?"

"I am."

Jack moved on, feeling a little hurt by her distance, but understanding regardless. He suddenly felt alone, and a little lost. If he wasn't with Gwen, he wasn't with her friends either… and he hadn't spoken with any of his old friends in weeks. He walked the halls alone, making his way to his first class while trying to cheer himself up. But the questions still lingered in his head, what if Jill never forgave him? What if he was to finish his senior year all alone?

When time for recess came, he made his way to Jill's locker as fast as he could, and slipped a note inside. He'd gotten one of the girls at his class to write it so Jill wouldn't recognize his handwriting, and he hoped she'd be curious enough to show up.

"I know your secret. Come talk to me under the bleachers after class," the note read. He had no clue if she had any secrets, but knowing Jill, she'd be curious enough to show up.

He spent the rest of the day on his own, jumping from class to class while his heart threatened to jump off his chest. He sat around the corner from the main doors when school ended and watched Jill as she walked out of the building and said goodbye to Justin, then Ronan and Penelope. She stood by the doors for a minute, looking around her bag until she got her car keys out.

"Please, don't go, please, please, please," Jack pleaded from a few feet away, hoping Jill had seen the note.

The lot started to empty out, and Jill stood there, getting things out of her bag and putting them back in. When the bus was gone and the place had cleared of half the students, Jill headed back into the training fields with slow steps. He waited a minute before going around the other side of the building, not wanting it to look like he was following her. By the time he rounded the corner, he saw her there, standing under the bleachers with a stone-hard face. She had her arms closed over her chest, her foot tapping on the floor the way she did whenever she was angry.

Not a great start.

Jack walked towards her slowly, and the moment she saw him, the world seemed to stop. They stood a few feet away, alone in the school grounds, the wind blowing softly and bringing her usual perfume all the way to Jack's nostrils.

God, he'd missed her. He walked the distance between them, and dropped to his knees in front of her. Jill didn't even reach his shoulder, and Jack didn't want to be above her for this, he certainly felt like he belonged below. Without leaving any space for complaints, he started talking before Jill could run away.

"I'm so sorry, Jill," he said, "I have wronged you in the worst possible way, and I have regretted my words every single day since. I understand if you can't forgive me, for what I did was horrible. But please, know that I am utterly, completely, and irrevocably sorry for what I did and the way I acted. You are and have always been the best friend I have ever had, you were there when I needed you, every single time, and I didn't know how to be there for you. And… I don't know if you can forgive me, but if you find it in your heart to do so, then I will live the rest of my life making sure I make this up to you. Jill… you deserve better."

Halfway down his speech, Jack had dropped his head down, looking at the ground below, too ashamed to look at Jill in the eyes. He noticed she was clutching his note in one fisted hand, and when the silence stretched, he finally dared to look back up.

Jill's eyes looked puffy as she opened and closed her mouth.

"You're damn right, I do deserve better. You broke me, Jack," she finally said. "You've been there by my side since the very start, and you know how much of a shit I give about people talking down on me, joking because of my size, or my shape, I couldn't care less!" She was gesturing with her arms, her voice raised to almost yelling. "But you… *you*," her voice dropped so low that Jack straightened his back to be closer to her. "You're the only one that has the power to break me, and I hate you for that," she finished, looking away.

"Jill…"

Jack's throat felt tight with the anguish he saw in her eyes, and he was unable to keep his truths in for any longer. Every single lie he had told himself shattered as he looked into her mossy green eyes and he let it all out.

"I want you to listen very closely," he said slowly, waiting until she looked at him in the eyes, "I'm a stupid ass that has never said this out loud before even if I've thought about it every single day since I met you… You. Are. Beautiful."

He accentuated every single word, letting them hang in the air between them. Jill looked almost confused, as if unsure of what to say or do. Jack lifted a hand slowly, and brushed a curl of her hair behind her ear.

"Everything about you, is amazing. I have been in awe of you my whole life. I wish I could be as strong willed as you are. Wished I could have been strong enough to defend you instead of just sit by, but I will do better. And my chest hurts thinking you might not want me to be a part of your life anymore, because I am lost without you."

Jill bit her lip, looking down at him while shaking her head.

"Jill, I... I love you," he choked out, and stared at her in shock after he said it. He couldn't even believe it himself. *He had known.* He'd known it for so long, but it had been so easy to deny it. It had been so easy to be too scared with the excuse that admitting his feelings could end their friendship. But he'd already lost her, he'd lost all hope and lost his best friend —so there was nothing else to lose.

"Do you mean that?" Her arms were still crossed, her face stoic, but there was a small twist to her lips that Jack knew very well.

"I meant every single word that I've said. I love the way you tease me, because you know it makes me stronger. I love the way you defend me, because you know I need to learn by example so I can do it myself. I love how you don't give a crap about what people think, because you are true to who you are. And I love the way you're trying so hard not to smile right now... you're probably about to make your lip bleed." Jack dared reach out and run his thumb through the swollen lip. "Stop biting it," he said softly. "You don't have to mask with me."

She didn't reject his touch, but she didn't lean into it either. She stood her ground, looking at him up and down as if trying to figure out the best course of action. After what felt like forever, she smiled.

"I'm not forgiving you because you deserve it, you'll still have to make it up to me every damn day. I'm forgiving you because I've fucking missed you, and there's so much I've wanted to share with you and couldn't, and you're an ass, Jack Wicks, but I have been stupidly in love with you since the day I saw you peeing on that tree in your front yard," she said while laughing.

She wiped the single tear that was rolling down her cheek, and leaned down, grabbing both sides of his face and pressing her lips against his.

CHAPTER 7

The night was warm and clear as Jack crossed the road into Jill's house wearing his tuxedo. He felt oddly out of place, but there was no other way he'd rather have it. Having his best friend back in his life had been a blessing, but having her as a girlfriend? Jack's life had gone from being a mess, to being the best thing ever almost overnight. Jill had still given him grief every day for how badly he had treated her, but it was in her usual joke-kind of way.

After that first kiss, Jack and Jill had talked about everything and anything. They had stayed under the bleachers until the sun had gone down, getting up to speed with each other's lives. Jack had told her the story of everything that had happened with Gwen, and how he knew she wasn't the one for him. And Jill had finally told Jack that she had been thinking about modeling and was looking to go to fashion school after graduation.

Jack hadn't been brave enough to ask her about the guy he had seen at her place, but he guessed it was not his place. If Jill had been with someone while he had been with Gwen, who was him to judge her? So imagine his surprise when he got to Jill's door on prom night, his tux perfectly in place, a bouquet of flowers in his hands, and before he could knock, the door opened up.

"Thank you for everything, Mrs. Williams," a tall and handsome guy was saying, making his way out the door.

Jack took a step back not to be ran into, and his jaw dropped. It was the guy from that night. The perfect magazine smile guy. And he was at Jill's place —on prom night.

"Oh, Jack, so glad you're here, Jill is in the lounge, come on, come inside," Sarah encouraged him.

What was going on?

"Oh, is this Jack? The boyfriend?" Mr. Perfect asked.

"Yes, I am… And who are you?" Jack dared ask.

"How rude, excuse me," he put his hand forward for a shake. "I'm Jackson Frasher, Jill's agent."

"Agent?"

His question became irrelevant the second he heard a voice inside the house, and looked over Jackson's shoulder. Jill was walking towards the door, her hair pinned up with only two loose curls framing her face. She was wearing a bit of makeup that made her eyes look greener, and her lips thicker. And the dress. *Oh, the dress.*

"You look… stunning," Jack said, not being able to contain the smile of joy at how gorgeous and happy Jill looked.

"You clean up alright yourself," Jill joked. "I see you've met Jackson. Sorry I didn't tell you about this before… Jackson is my modeling agent, he actually… he just got me my first gig, and that's why he came over to tell me about it." Jill looked almost shy, which was so out of character, Jack couldn't help a nervous giggle.

"What?" he looked back and forth between Jackson, Sarah, and Jill, unable to believe what he was hearing. *His girlfriend had officially become a model?* "Oh, damn, I'm so proud of you!" he finally yelled, rushing to her side and hugging her tightly. He placed a kiss on her forehead, not wanting to ruin her makeup, and Jill squeezed him back, her smile so bright it could have blinded him.

A honk sounded at the door, and they all turned around in time to see Penelope, Ronan and Justin poking their heads out of the limousine.

"You better go kids, have fun!" Sarah said while pushing them out the door.

Jack and Jill danced the night away with their friend ——the old and the new. Gwen had come around at some point, congratulated Jill for her amazing gown, and then the three of them had danced together for a while before Gwen had returned to her date. They had danced together, in groups, and they even slow-danced when the time came.

The night was as magical as it should have been, and everything was finally in place. Jack had everything he'd ever dreamed of—or almost.

"Can't believe the year is almost over," Jack said while they sat down at the bleachers in the school's gym.

Jill was sitting by his side, and suddenly, she moved over and sat sideways on Jack's lap, the same way she'd done so many times since they've been kids. It left their faces at the same height now, and Jack couldn't help himself, pressing a kiss to his girl's lips, which turned into passionate kissing in no time. Jill had her arms around Jack's shoulders and he felt her chest pressing against him, sending shivers down his spine.

"It's been a rollercoaster of a year, hasn't it?" Jill replied when they took a breather after a few minutes.

The room felt hot, and Jack felt his blood draining down as it had done so many times before when having Jill so close. He almost felt lightheaded, and he chuckled.

"And after all of it, I will still finish off school without getting laid," he joked.

"I can change that," Jill said, a playful smile twisting her lips. The room was dimly lit, and Jill's puffy skirt was fanning around both of them, enough so to hide them from prying eyes when Jill brough her hand down to Jack's crotch.

"Wow," Jack jumped, looking around nervously.

"And I can see you're quite ready for it," Jill's smile was devilish, and Jack couldn't help but grin.

"Are you sure about what you're offering?"

"Let's get out of here," was Jill's only answer as she got to her feet and dragged Jack behind her.

She walked quickly, and Jack had no issue following her steps with his long legs. "Where are you taking me?" he asked, looking around to the empty halls they were walking, heading into the depths of the school.

"To a room no one ever uses," she said with a crooked grin.

She led them to the counselor's office, and Jack's jaw dropped when Jill grabbed a key hidden on the frame of the door and opened it up.

"How did you—"

"Me and Mrs. Green are good friends," she replied with a shrug, "I've been coming here almost every day since we started high school," she admitted.

It made so much sense, that Jack couldn't do more than hold her between his arms. This woman was the strongest person he'd ever known, and he was beyond lucky to be able to call her his girl-friend.

"I'm proud of you," he whispered in her ear as Jill locked the door and closed the blinds.

"Oh, damn you, Jack, you know how to turn on a girl with simple words."

She pushed Jack towards a couch on the corner of the room with her palms on his chest. "If it's okay with you, I might do this rough and fast... there will be plenty of time for sweet and slow... but right now, I really have the urge to devour you."

Jill's hands were already undoing the buttons of his shirt as she spoke, and Jack couldn't do much more than nod his agreement before her lips crushed against his. She kissed him like she'd never done before, their hands exploring each other in ways they haven't yet tried. It was just the two of them, the same way it had ever been, and they let every insecurity, every problem and every disagreement they ever had be forgotten as they lost themselves in the folds of their skins and the warmth of their touch.

Jill guided Jack down until he was on his back, and she straddled on top of him, kissing his bare chest, his neck, savoring every bit of skin she could find.

"You are beautiful," Jack breathed, his eyes glassy as he looked at her in awe, his hands exploring her curves and helping her get the dress over her head.

Jill believed him, and she made it known in the way she rode him, loving every inch of him the same way he loved every inch of her. Bare, naked, exposed. They were one, they were imperfect, but perfect in the way they molded to each other. They were loved, and inexperience didn't matter when all they wanted was to make each other feel alive and cared for. Jack's first time was rushed, greedy, but perfect. And the second... well, the second was even better.

EPILOGUE

The dorm is smaller than what Jack imagined, but he can't complain. He's at the college he had as his first choice, he's not too far away from home, and everything he cares about is no further than a train ride away. He's almost done unpacking, only one box to go, when his phone starts ringing.

"Who's calling you at this time?" Russell, his new friend and roommate asks as he comes closer.

"I think I know who," he mumbles. It's pretty late in the night, which can only mean one person.

Jack looks for his phone between the clothes thrown about on his bed, until the lit screen is looking back at him. Right there under the caller ID there's a picture of a model, her blond curls falling around her shoulders while she holds a margarita in one hand. There's a beautiful beach behind her and she's wearing a lovely two piece swimsuit.

"I knew it," Jack says with a huge and proud smile on his face as he shows Russell the picture on the screen, "It's my girlfriend."

www.ingramcontent.com/pod-product-compliance
Lightning Source LLC
Chambersburg PA
CBHW060914130726
48001CB00006B/2232